A NOT SCARY Story About BIG SCARY Things

C.K. Williams

Illustrated by

Gabi Swiatkowska

HARCOURT CHILDREN'S BOOKS
Houghton Mifflin Harcourt
Boston New York 2010

Harcourt Children's Books is an imprint of Houghton Mifflin Harcourt Publishing Company.
www.hmhbooks.com

The illustrations in this book were done with water-based paints on paper.
The text type was set in Letterpress, Infiltro, and Monster Font.
The display type was set in Monster Font.
Designed by Christine Kettner and Elynn Cohen

Library of Congress Cataloging-in-Publication Data
Williams, C. K. (Charles Kenneth), 1936-
A not scary story about big scary things / C. K. Williams ; illustrated by Gabi Swiatkowska.
p. cm.
Summary: A little boy walking through an ordinary forest encounters an extraordinary monster.
ISBN 978-0-15-205466-3 (hardcover : alk. paper)
[1. Monsters—Fiction. 2. Fear—Fiction.] I. Swiatkowska, Gabi, ill. II. Title.
PZ7.W655886No 2010
[E]—dc22
2009036540

Manufactured in China
LEO 10 9 8 7 6 5 4 3 2 1
4500220978

Once upon a time there was a forest.

It was your regular, ordinary, standard sort of forest. It had big dark trees that blocked the sunlight. It had hills and mountains that you had to climb. It had cliffs to fall off and rivers to fall in. And also, you knew that probably in this forest were bears who growled: you could tell because if you listened *very* hard you could almost hear them. And there also might have been wolves who howled, because you could *almost* hear them, too. And probably there were big snakes that slithered through the underbrush right next to the path.

In short, it was your usual scary, frightening, terrifying, mystifying forest.

Except.

Except that this forest was a little different from other forests because along with all those other scary things—the bears and wolves and snakes and cliffs—it had one other thing: it had a **MONSTER!**

That's what people said, anyway. People said there was a monster in that forest. It was awful, they said. It was big—about ten feet, six inches tall. And it was scary. It was green, for one thing. Or blue. Or maybe it changed colors. It had long, sharp claws, for another thing.

And TEETH!

And FANGS!

BIG long, sharp FANGS. And a BIG prickly tail BIGGER

like a PORCUPINE'S, but much BIGGER and sharper.

And people said that this monster liked nothing better in the world than to scare little children.

TO REALLY SCARE LITTLE CHILDREN!

Now, one day there was just such a child walking through the forest. It was a little boy. What in heaven's name do you think he was doing alone in that scary forest?

Well, maybe he had an errand to do.

Maybe he had to take this or that from here to there.

here

there

Or maybe that or this had to go from there to here.

here

Who knows?

there

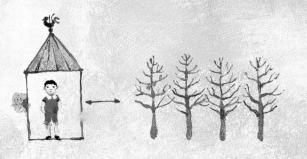 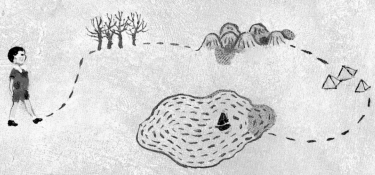

Maybe he just lived near the forest.　　Maybe he was just taking a walk.

It doesn't matter.

There he was, in the forest, walking along the path alone under the big dark trees.

But even though this was a scary, frightening, TERRIFYING forest,

this little boy wasn't afraid.

He was pretty sure that he could hear
the bears growling in their caves,

but he knew that all bears like to do anyway is
to eat fish and berries and to take naps.
He thought he could hear wolves howling, too,

but he knew that wolves liked to stay as far away as they could from human beings so that they could hunt and howl hello to each other.

What about snakes, though?

Well, the little boy knew that snakes were more afraid of people than people were of snakes and that even if you saw one, all you had to do was stop and wait and the snake would slither away from you.

And the monster?

The monster people said was in this forest?

The monster who was **ten feet,** six inches **tall?**

Who was green, or blue, or could change colors, and who had **BIG** long claws, and teeth and fangs?

What about the monster who went **RROWWL** and who just might be leaping out of the bushes at **you**?

WHAT ABOUT THE MONSTER WHO WAS LEAPING OUT AT YOU AND GOING **RROWWL** RIGHT NOW?

What do you do when *that* happens?

What this little boy did was that he didn't do anything. He just kept walking along the path. The big green or blue scary monster looked down at the little boy and crashed his fangs together and went "RROWWL," but the little boy just looked at him and kept walking. "RROWWL," the monster went again. The little boy looked at him again and just kept right on walking along the path that led through the forest back to his house.

Then the monster started jumping up and down alongside him.
He growled and RROWWLED again: "RROWWL."
He crashed his fangs together. He scrunched his claws into the ground.
He waved his prickly tail.

But the boy just walked along as though there weren't anybody there at all.

"Hey," the monster said finally, "you'd better
watch out, because if you're not careful
I might eat you up!"
The little boy just kept walking.
"RROWWL," the monster said.
"Hey, you're supposed to be afraid of me.
Aren't you afraid of me?"
"No, I'm not," the little boy said.
"What do you mean?" the monster asked.
"Look at how huge I am. Look at how scary
I am. Watch—I'll crash my fangs for you."
"I don't care," the boy said.
"I'm not afraid of you, because I don't believe in you."

"You don't *believe* in me?" the monster said. "But I'm right here in front of you. Don't you see how scary I am? Everybody says I'm scary."

"I don't care what everybody says," the little boy said. "You're not real. Monsters aren't real."

"I'm not *real?*" the monster asked. "Look." And he thrashed his big tail in the bushes.

"That doesn't make you real," the little boy said.

"Listen," said the monster. "I'll crash my fangs *really loud for you.*" And he did:

CRASH!

"I don't care," the boy said. "You're not real. The bear growling in his cave is real, but he won't bother anybody, and the wolves howling far away are real, and the snake slithering along the ground who's actually afraid of everything and everybody is real, but you—

you're just not **real**."

"Look," the monster said. "I'll change colors for you. Then you'll see I'm real." And he changed from green to blue to red to green and back again. But the little boy just kept walking along.

"Watch now: I'll make my teeth even longer and sharper for you," the monster said.

And his teeth got longer and sharper and his fangs CRASHED EVEN LOUDER, but the little boy just kept walking along.

He was almost home now and he was a little hungry, so he
started walking faster.

"Wait," the monster said. "What am I supposed to do if
you don't believe in me? That's my *job*, you know. That's
what I'm supposed to *do*: SCARE boys and girls."

"I'm sorry," the boy answered, "but I can't believe in something
that's not real."

The monster was very upset now. "Couldn't you believe in me just a little bit?" he asked the boy.

If you had been there when he said that, you'd probably have been a little surprised and looked at the monster even more closely, because you might have thought that the monster was suddenly a bit smaller than he had been before.

"Nope," the boy said.

"Please," the monster begged. "Couldn't you believe in me just a teeny bit?"

The monster definitely was smaller now. He wasn't even close to ten feet, six inches tall. In fact, he was only about six feet . . . No, even less than that. Why, he wasn't any bigger than the little boy.

"Just a teeny, weeny little bit?" the monster begged again.

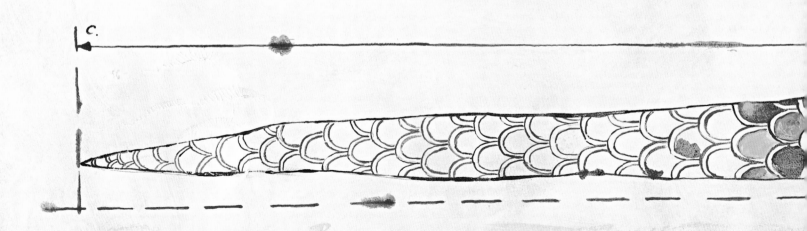

a.

y.

MONSTER

d.

x.

b.

the boy.

6

5

4,5

4

3

2

1

0

The monster was much smaller now.
He was so small in fact that he was
having trouble keeping up with the boy.
The boy was nearly home; it was almost
dinnertime, and he was even hungrier
than before, so he was going pretty fast.

"Hey, wait up!" the monster
said. "Don't leave me all alone out
here like this."

"Okay," the little boy said, and he picked up the monster.

The monster nestled in the boy's arms. He was so small now that he looked very much like a kitten.

"Please, please," he said, "please believe in me a little bit."

"Well, all right," the boy said. "I suppose I could believe in you a little, but no more than that."

Just then, the boy arrived home. There was his mother standing on the steps of their house.

"Look what I found in the forest," the boy said, and he lifted up the monster in his arms to show his mother.

"Meow," the monster said. "Meow. Meow."
"Please, Mom," the little boy said, "can I keep him?"